A TEMPLAR BOOK

Produced by The Templar Company plc,
Pippbrook Mill, London Road, Dorking, Surrey RH4 1JE, Great Britain.

Text copyright © *A Tale of Shuffle, Trot and Merry* 1926-1953 by Darrell Waters Limited
Illustration and design copyright © 1994 by The Templar Company plc
Enid Blyton's signature mark is a registered trademark of Darrell Waters Limited

This edition produced for Parragon Books,
Unit 13-17, Avonbridge Trading Estate, Atlantic Road, Avonmouth, Bristol BS11 9QD

This book contains material first published as
A Tale of Shuffle, Trot and Merry in Enid Blyton's Sunny Stories
and Sunny Stories between 1926 and 1953.

Illustrated by Kate Davies

Printed and bound in Italy

ISBN 1 85813 667 9

Enid Blyton's

POCKET LIBRARY

A Tale of Shuffle, Trot and Merry

Illustrated by Kate Davies

PARRAGON

"Now come along!" shouted Mr Smarty. "Where are you, Shuffle, Trot and Merry? I've some shopping here ready for you to take to my house!"

They were playing marbles in a corner of the market.

Shuffle groaned. "Blow! Now we've got to put his sacks of shopping on our backs and walk for miles to his house. I'm tired of it! Why doesn't he buy a horse and cart for us to drive?"

"Because it's too expensive," said Trot. "Come along – he'll be cross if we don't hurry."

They went over to Mr Smarty, who was standing by three big sacks.

"Oh – so there you are, you lazy lot!" he said. "I've bought all these things at the market, and I want them taken to my house as fast as possible."

"It's too hot to walk fast with big sacks like those!" said Shuffle.

"We won't get there before midnight," said Trot, gloomily.

"Well – I'll do my best," said Merry.

"I'll give a gold piece to the one who gets to my house first," said Mr Smarty.

They pricked up their ears at that! A gold piece! That was riches to them.

Sly old Shuffle went over to the sacks at once, and quickly felt them all. Oh – what a heavy one – and the second was heavy too – but the third one felt as light as a feather! That was the one for him!

"I shall hardly know I've a sack on my back!" he thought. "I'll easily be the first one there and I'll get the gold piece!"

He shuffled off with the very light sack on his back.

Trot went over to the two sacks left, wondering what was in them.

He stuck a finger into one – it was
full of something round and hard –
potatoes, perhaps? He stuck a
finger into the other and felt

something loose and soft – what
was it – flour – salt – sugar? He
pulled out his finger and sucked it.
It tasted sweet and delicious.

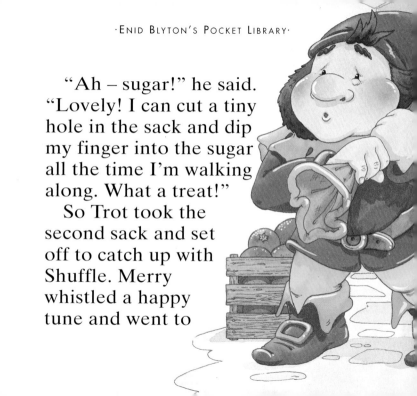

"Ah – sugar!" he said. "Lovely! I can cut a tiny hole in the sack and dip my finger into the sugar all the time I'm walking along. What a treat!"

So Trot took the second sack and set off to catch up with Shuffle. Merry whistled a happy tune and went to

the sack that was left. He made a face as he lifted it on to his back. "It's heavy – full of potatoes, I think – probably covered in mud too, which makes them twice as heavy. Well – here goes – I must catch up Shuffle and Trot before they get too far, or I won't win that gold piece!"

But it was difficult to catch up with Shuffle, even though he was not the fastest walker as a rule – because his sack was so very, very light. Shuffle had no idea what was inside, and he didn't care. He was delighted to have picked such a light load!

"That gold piece is as good as in my pocket!" he thought. "And

I'm going to keep it all for myself!"

Trot was having quite a good time with his sack, as he trotted along eating the sugar. What a joke, he thought – he was lightening his load and having a feast at the same time!

Merry walked fast, but his load was really heavy – and then he had the bad luck to stub his toe on a big stone, and that made him limp!

"Just my luck!" he groaned. "I'll never catch up with the others now – I can't walk fast with a sore toe!" So Merry fell behind, but all the same he whistled a merry tune and smiled at anyone he passed. But soon clouds began to cover the sun,

and a wind blew up and made the trees sway to and fro. Then Merry felt a drop of rain on his face and he sighed.

"Now it's going to pour with rain and I shall get soaked. I'd better give up all hope of getting that gold piece!"

The rain began to pelt down, stinging the faces of the three little fellows. Shuffle was a great way ahead of the others, and he grinned as he looked round and saw how far behind they were.

But, as the rain poured down, odd things began to happen! First of all, Shuffle's sack grew heavier!

"Is my sack getting heavy, or am I just imagining it?" he thought.

He walked a little further and then felt that he must have a rest. "My sack feels twice as heavy! Whatever can be inside?" He set it down and untied the rope.

He put in his hand and felt something soft, squashy and wet! The rain had gone right into the sack. Can you guess what it was inside?

It was a sponge! "No wonder the sack felt so light when the sponges were dry!" said Shuffle, in dismay. "Now they're soaked with rain and as heavy as can be! What can I do?"

Trot came along grinning. "Hello Shuffle – so your load was sponges, was it? It serves you right for

picking the lightest load as usual.
Now you've got the heaviest!"

"What's in your sack?"
called Shuffle, annoyed,
but Trot didn't stop.
No, he saw a chance
of winning that
gold piece now.
He was going
quite fast.
Also his sack
felt lighter!

In fact, it soon felt so light that Trot stopped in surprise. "What's happening?" he thought. "My sack feels remarkably light!"

He set it down to see – and, to his horror, he found that the sugar was all melting in the rain and dripping fast out of the bottom of the sack!

"I ought to get under cover, or it will all be melted away," thought Trot, in dismay. "Why didn't I remember that sugar melts? Well,

I've outpaced old Shuffle – but if I wait till the rain stops Merry will be sure to catch me up and pass me, and I shan't get that gold piece."

So on he went in the pouring rain, while the sugar in his sack melted faster than ever. But at least he was now in the lead!

As for Merry he still whistled in the pouring rain, for he was a light-hearted fellow. The rain ran into his sack, down among the potatoes and soon muddy water was dripping out at the bottom. Merry laughed.

"You're washing all the dirty potatoes for me!" he said to the rain clouds above. "Hello – there's Shuffle in front of me – he's very slow today!"

He soon passed Shuffle, who groaned loudly as Merry passed him. "My load is sponges!" he shouted. "And they're four times

as heavy as they were now that they're soaked with rain."

"Serves you right!" said Merry. "You picked the lightest sack so that you could win that gold piece!"

The three went on through the rain, and at last came one by one to Mr Smarty's big house. Trot arrived at the back door first and set down his sack on the ground.

"Hello!" said the cook. "Have you brought something for the master?

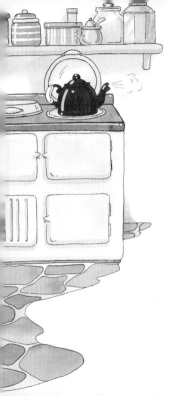

"I'll tell him you were the first to arrive."

The next was Merry with his sack of potatoes. The cook peered at them and smiled. "Well I never – the potatoes are all washed clean for me! That's a good mark for you, Merry."

Last of all came poor Shuffle, very weary with carrying such a wet and heavy load. He set his sack down and water from the sponges ran all over the floor.

"Now pick up that sack and stand it outside!" said the cook. "My floor's in enough mess already without you making it a running river. What in the world have you got in that sack?"

But Shuffle was too tired to answer. The cook gave them all some food

and drink and they sat back and waited to be seen by Mr Smarty.

At last they were sent for, and the cook took them in to his study.

"Here's the one who arrived first," she said, pushing Trot forward. His sack looked limp, wet and empty. Mr Smarty glared at it in rage.

"What's this? It should be full of sugar! Where's the sugar, Trot? Have you sold it to someone on the way?"

"No, sir. The rain melted it," said Trot. "I was here first, sir. Can I have my gold piece?"

"Bah! You don't deserve it." said Mr Smarty. "Why didn't you get under cover and save my expensive sugar?" Then he turned to Shuffle.

"Shuffle, you were third, so you're out of it. Take that disgustingly dripping sack out of the room. Merry, what about you?"

"Sir, he's brought potatoes – and they're all washed clean!" said the cook, eagerly, for she liked Merry. "He deserves the gold piece, even though he wasn't the first here!"

Merry laughed. "The rain did the cleaning!" he said.

"You weren't the first," said Mr Smarty, "but you certainly delivered my goods in a better condition

than when I bought them – so I shall award the gold piece for that." He tossed a shining coin to the delighted Merry, who went happily off to the kitchen. What sulks and grumbles met him from Shuffle and Trot! He clapped them on the shoulder.

"Cheer up – we'll go and spend my gold piece together. What's good luck for but to be shared!"

They all went out arm in arm and the cook stared after them, smiling.

"You deserve good luck, Merry!" she called. "And you'll always get it – a merry face and a generous heart are the luckiest things in the world!"

I think she could be right.